Lydia R.

Treasure Map

Finding Your Own
Treasures in the Scriptures

To God be the Glory!

Ruth E. Wiertzema

Book One - Lydia

A Bible Study by

Ruth A. Wiertzema

CRM BOOKS
P.O. Box 2124
Hendersonville, NC 28793

Visit our Web site at www.ciridmus.com

Printed in the United States of America

10-digit ISBN: 1-933341-14-9
13-digit ISBN: 978-1-933341-4-9

LCCN: 2006925446

Lydia Ruth's Treasure Map

Finding Your Own Treasures in the Scriptures

Book One - Lydia

A Bible Study by

Ruth A. Wiertzema

CRM BOOKS
Publishing Hope for Today's Society
Inspirational Books~CDs~Children's Books~Cards & Gift Art

To Catherine,

a treasure from God,
whose joyful exuberance and
adventuresome heart
enticed me to finally
begin my journey.

Acknowledgments

To Rose King, who graciously pondered with me over my ponderings, which set the compass for this journey.

To Arlene Groen and Millie Lais, sisters by birth, and Karen Evers and Fran Holmblad, sisters of the heart, whose love and encouragement gave me bread for the journey.

To Jeanette Greeley, "Somethin' Else", whose generous heart turns dreams into realities.

To Revelle Lawson, who tested this study as it unfolded, and focused her technical wizardry on organizing the manuscript.

Lydia Ruth's Treasure Map

grew out of the LIFT UP MINE EYES SERIES-7 historical fiction volumes by Catherine Ritch Guess-based on real-life missionaries John and Imogene Barden of eastern North Carolina who served the Belgian Congo during the 1920's and 30's. Though the Barden's true story is told through the eyes of a fictional character, Lydia Mason, Guess recognized the need for readers, who like her character Lydia, had little or no knowledge of the Bible or how to discover its greatest riches. She knew that Ruth A. Wiertzema was the person to write that study of 6 books.

CRM BOOKS wishes to thank Ruth for her knowledge, expertise and dedication not only to *Lydia Ruth's Treasure Map*, but in her work with others around the country. Most especially, we appreciate the love with which she pursues each of her endeavors.

INTRODUCTION

Every person has the opportunity to receive his or her **own** personal message from the Bible.

Finding our own message from God in the Scriptures does, however, require effort. The Bible is sometimes difficult to read and understand. There is a "language problem". The original Hebrew and Greek words do not translate easily into English. Over the years, scholars have worked to render better translations and interpretations until we now have an almost endless array of Bibles and study aides from which to choose. Yet, people still find Bible study a challenge.

I was first introduced to Bible study at the age of nine when I began catechism training. While it was basically a doctrinal training, each "question" that we memorized also required memorization of a supporting Scripture verse. This was not accomplished without a good bit of agony. Picture me, standing on a "concentration chair" while my mother "examined" me before class. It wasn't until years later that I saw the wisdom in her method; she well knew standing on that chair I could go nowhere and would stay focused.

At thirteen, I advanced into confirmation class and was then taught how to use Bible study helps. Classes were held at the parsonage and taught by the pastor and his wife. Classes were rigorous, to say the least. Along with the confirmation book we had extra assignments such as hand drawing the maps of Paul's missionary journeys. I still have those drawings. We sat at the big dining room table. The design in the lace tablecloth is still indelibly etched in my mind to this day. How often I stared into it, hoping there would be some clue there on days when I had not prepared well.

Regular attendance in Sunday school and worship all through my growing years and into adulthood exposed me to more of the Scriptures. I am eternally grateful for the blessing of this background that set the foundations of my faith development. It established a life-long desire to study the Scriptures.

Yet, to a large degree, the message that I received from the Scripture was not necessarily my own. It was filtered through the words and interpretations of others. Gradually, I began to realize that I had plenty of "head knowledge". I knew much **about** the Scripture. Lacking was real "heart knowledge". What was God's message for ME? How did I connect the Biblical story to my present-day life? I began to realize that the words in the Bible had to move from information to transformation. But how would I go about truly connecting "The Story" with "my story"?

No one else can do it for us. Each of us must do our own pondering, searching and listening. When we are willing to do so, we will hear God speaking to us, personally. The treasures are there, waiting.

My prayer is that as you follow this map, you will discover your own treasures – your own messages from God in the Scriptures – and that your life will change because of it.

To God be the Glory!

uth A. Wiertzema

Find the city of Philippi, the home of Lydia, where Paul visited on his second missionary journey

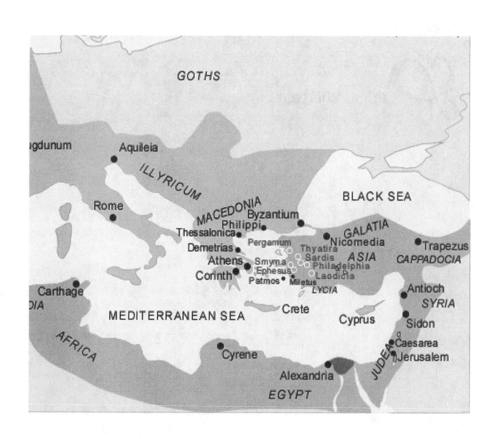

Where Will the Treasure Map Take Me?

✢ The Treasure Map will guide you in researching and pondering the Scriptures as you seek to
find God's word to you in the story of Lydia.

✢ The Treasure Map will guide you in learning to
tell and re-tell the Biblical story of Lydia.

✢ The Treasure Map will challenge you to apply
the treasures you find in the story of Lydia to
your own life.

*Seek not to understand that you
may believe; but believe that
you may understand.*
Saint Augustine (354-430)

What Will I Encounter on the Journey?

Reading & Re-reading

Research

Reflecting & Pondering

Recording

Retelling & Telling

Revelation

Reporting

Responding

Remembering

INTRODUCTION

How Will I Go About
This Treasure Search?

Invite two to four persons to share this journey with you. Each will need their own study guide. There are three sessions to this study. It is suggested that your group meet three consecutive weeks. If you have a larger group, divide into subgroups. The purpose is to allow space for all to be involved.

The Lydia Ruth's Treasure Map incorporates both individual and group study. It is <u>individual</u> in that you will be reading and pondering the Scripture, listening for God's message(s) for you, and recording learnings and insights. It is <u>group</u> in that along the way you will be sharing your discoveries with other travelers, as they will be sharing their discoveries with you.

Throughout your study, you are encouraged to use more than one Bible translation. You are also encouraged to use additional Bible study helps such as concordances, dictionaries, encyclopedias or atlases to better understand the setting and context of the Biblical story or to understand difficult or Bible-specific words.

However, **please wait to use Bible <u>commentaries</u> until you have completed your own treasure search and discovered your own message.** Then you will be ready to hear the message through other voices.

Study helps are usually available for use from a church or pastor's library. They can also be purchased at any Christian bookstore.

> *On the following page is a short description of such resources. Any of these are now available as computer resources or on the World Wide Web.*

Tools to Help You Search

Recommended are the following general, basic resources to help you during your search:

Bible Atlas – contains detailed maps and graphics relating to Bible times.

Bible Concordance – contains alphabetical list of key words in the Bible and the scripture reference(s) where they appear.

Bible Dictionary – contains definitions of Bible names, places, terms and concepts.

Bible Encyclopedia – contains descriptions and visual illustrations of the settings, events, and people of Bible times.

Recommended after completing Session 3:

Study Bible – contains the Biblical text along with extra helps including explanatory notes and "comments".

Commentaries and Handbooks – contain a general overview of the Bible text with some "comments" on the scripture.

Context and Setting for the Story of Lydia

Acts 16:11 - 15

The writer (held to be Luke) of the Acts of the Apostles begins with the story of Jesus' ascension into Heaven at which time Jesus gave these instructions to his followers: "You will be my witnesses both in Jerusalem and all Judea and in Samaria and to the farthest bounds of earth". The work Jesus began was given into their hands to be continued. The Gospel was no longer to be confined to Jerusalem, nor to the Jews only, but was for all persons, everywhere.

A key character in the story of Lydia is Paul (Saul). As a Jewish religious leader (Saul), he had taken part in persecuting the followers of Jesus. The persecution caused many believers to leave Jerusalem and locate in other places. On his way to Damascus, he was blinded. The man sent to heal him told him about Jesus. He became a Christian (Paul), and began preaching the Gospel. Eventually he was sent by the early church believers as a missionary to spread the Gospel to other parts of the world.

The story of Lydia is found in the midst of Paul's second missionary journey. One of the cities visited was Philippi. Because of the small number of Jews in Philippi, there was no synagogue. People would gather at the river on the Sabbath to worship. Lydia was a "seller of purple" – rich cloth. She was obviously a successful businesswoman. She was a Gentile (non-Jew) but worshipped God, and was among those gathered for worship when Paul arrived at the river. Lydia was the first convert in Europe.

The story takes place about 20 years after Jesus' death and resurrection.

**The Treasure Map will guide you
in researching and pondering the Scriptures
as you seek to find God's word to you
in the story of Lydia.**

Session One

We live in an "instant" world where thoughts and images change every few seconds. This is counter to what we must discipline ourselves to do when seeking our own message from God through the Scriptures.

The search requires prayer. It requires guidance from the Holy Spirit. It requires an open heart; an open mind. It requires reading and *pondering* God's Word.

Along the way, you will encounter some unknowns that may require extra research before you can continue your journey. You will not find your treasure in the first mile. The journey itself, taken step by step, will lead you to rich discoveries.

For at least five days, read and "ponder" **Acts 16:11-15**. Pondering may be a new concept – it simply means to take time with the Scripture. Let it flow through your thinking; your imagination; your heart. To do this you will want to read and re-read the verses. It takes more than one or two readings for the words to begin speaking to you.

Record your thoughts, insights and questions.

The butterfly icon will remind you to ponder throughout this week.

Each day there is also a suggested "pondering". Look for two butterflies.

DAY ONE

Before you open your Bible:

- ✝ Pray for an open heart and an open mind.
- ✝ Invite the Holy Spirit to guide you.

Open your Bible. Read, and re-read the Biblical passage Acts 16:11-15, allowing it to flow through you.

A treasure from the Bible:
"Again, the kingdom of heaven is like
a merchant looking for fine pearls."
Matthew 13:45 NIV

Record thoughts from your ponderings:

Today's Date:_____

_____

_____

_____

_____

_____

_____

_____

_____

_____

_____

_____

_____

_____

_____

SESSION ONE: Day One

What words do I need to research to better understand?

_____

_____

_____

_____

_____

_____

_____

_____

_____

_____

_____

_____

_____

_____

_____

DAY TWO

Before you open your Bible:

- ✙ Pray for an open heart and an open mind.
- ✙ Invite the Holy Spirit to guide you.

Open your Bible. Read, and re-read the Biblical passage Acts 16:11-15, allowing it to flow through you.

A treasure from the Bible:

"With my whole heart I seek you; do not let me stray from your commands. I treasure your word in my heart that I may not sin against you. Blessed are you, O Lord, teach me your statutes."

Psalms 119:10 - 12 NRSV

Record thoughts from your ponderings:

Today's Date:_____

_____

_____

_____

_____

_____

_____

_____

_____

_____

_____

_____

_____

_____

_____

_____

SESSION ONE: Day Two

_____

_____

_____

_____

_____

_____

_____

_____

_____

_____

_____

_____

_____

_____

_____

_____

_____

_____

What did you "hear", "see", and "smell" when you read this passage?

_____

_____

_____

_____

_____

_____

_____

_____

_____

_____

_____

_____

_____

DAY THREE

Before you open your Bible:

✝ Pray for an open heart and an open mind.

✝ Invite the Holy Spirit to guide you.

Open your Bible. Read, and re-read the Biblical passage Acts 16:11-15, allowing it to flow through you.

A treasure from the Bible:

*"The kingdom of heaven is like
treasure hidden in a field. When
a man found it, he hid it again, and
then in his joy went and sold
all he had and bought that field."*

Matthew 13:44 NIV

Record thoughts from your ponderings:

Today's Date:_____

_____

_____

_____

_____

_____

_____

_____

_____

_____

_____

_____

_____

_____

_____

_____

SESSION ONE: Day Three

_____

_____

_____

_____

_____

_____

_____

_____

_____

_____

_____

_____

_____

_____

_____

_____

What actions took place in this passage?

_____

_____

_____

_____

_____

_____

_____

_____

_____

_____

_____

_____

_____

_____

_____

DAY FOUR

Before you open your Bible:

- ✛ Pray for an open heart and an open mind.
- ✛ Invite the Holy Spirit to guide you.

Open your Bible. Read, and re-read the Biblical passage Acts 16:11-15, allowing it to flow through you.

A treasure from the Bible:
"For where your treasure is, there
your heart will be also."
Luke 12:34 NIV

Record thoughts from your ponderings:

Today's Date:_____

_____

_____

_____

_____

_____

_____

_____

_____

_____

_____

_____

_____

_____

_____

_____

SESSION ONE: Day Four

What puzzles you in this story? What surprises you in this story?

_____

_____

_____

_____

_____

_____

_____

_____

_____

_____

_____

_____

_____

DAY FIVE

Before you open your Bible:

- ✝ Pray for an open heart and an open mind.
- ✝ Invite the Holy Spirit to guide you.

Open your Bible. Read, and re-read the Biblical passage Acts 16:11-15, allowing it to flow through you.

A treasure from the Bible:

"Jesus, looking at him, loved him and said, 'You lack one thing; go, sell what you own, and give the money to the poor, and you will have treasure in heaven; then come, follow me.'"

Mark 10:21 NRSV

Record thoughts from your ponderings:

Today's Date:_____

_____

_____

_____

_____

_____

_____

_____

_____

_____

_____

_____

_____

_____

_____

_____

SESSION ONE: Day Five

With whom do you most identify in this story? Why?

_____

_____

_____

_____

_____

_____

_____

_____

_____

_____

_____

_____

_____

_____

_____

OPTIONAL: DAY SIX & DAY SEVEN

Great discoveries may not have appeared by this point. DO NOT be discouraged!

Continue to ponder **and listen; move on in the journey.**

Before you open your Bible:
- ✛ Pray for an open heart and an open mind.
- ✛ Invite the Holy Spirit to guide you.

Open your Bible. Read, and re-read the Biblical passage Acts 16:11-15, allowing it to flow through you.

A treasure from the Bible:

"Today the Lord has obtained your agreement: to be his treasured people, as he promised you, and to keep his commandments."
Deuteronomy 26:18 NRSV

Record thoughts from your ponderings:

Today's Date:_____

_____

_____

_____

_____

_____

_____

_____

_____

_____

_____

_____

_____

_____

_____

_____

_____

_____

_____

_____

_____

_____

_____

_____

_____

_____

_____

_____

_____

_____

_____

_____

Record thoughts from your ponderings:

Today's Date:_____

_____

_____

_____

_____

_____

_____

_____

_____

_____

_____

_____

_____

_____

_____

_____

_____

_____

_____

Group Time Session One

In this first group time, discipline yourselves primarily to focusing on the process itself and what you have learned about yourself in following it. Your journey has just begun; there are yet discoveries to make in the next two sessions.

When you gather:

Determine the total length of time the group will meet.

Look at the suggestions for sharing. Make choices together as to which you want to use. You may want to add your own to the list.

When you have made your choices, calculate the approximate time you will have for each, in order to include them all in the total time you have together. Assign a time-keeper to move the group to each next discussion.

Covenant with each other to be sure every participant has equal opportunity to share.

Agree to a signal to alert each other when someone becomes too lengthy and it is time for someone else to speak.

As you begin the sharing time:

Pray together, and ask the Holy Spirit to be among you.

Suggestions:

Share what each of you has learned about the process of "pondering".

Share what each of you has learned about "listening".

Share what each of you found to be most puzzling in the Scripture.

Share what each of you found to be most surprising in the Scripture.

Share who in the story each of you most identify with. Why?

_____

_____

_____

_____

_____

_____

My Sharing Time Discoveries

_____

_____

_____

_____

_____

_____

_____

_____

_____

_____

_____

_____

_____

_____

_____

_____

_____

_____

The Treasure Map will guide you in learning to tell, and to re-tell the Biblical story of Lydia.

Session Two

Finding a treasure from God is exciting, and something we want to share with others. However, I have come to believe that we must be able to tell "The Story" along with our own story; for it was *within* the Biblical story that *our* treasure – God's message to us – was found.

I learned the power of this combined witness from a dear friend and spiritual mentor in the mountains of southeastern Kentucky. Whenever she talked of God's guidance in her life, she would begin with "Like the story in Matthew about"....after which she would recount the actual Biblical story in her own words. The telling of the Biblical story was an introduction to what she would then say about some particular message or direction God was giving her. Through practice, we also can learn to effectively tell the Biblical story, and to connect that story to our story. In this session we will learn both to **tell** and to **re-tell** the story of Lydia.

At this point, you may be saying: "Me...a storyteller! You've got to be kidding!"

Good news for you....with practice, you **can** do it. In fact, you tell stories every day. The key word here is "practice.....practice.....practice". The more you do it, the more comfortable you will become.

TELLING

When we **tell** the Biblical story we must know it well enough for it to become our own. However, while we may change the words to our words, we do not change the story.

We may include information about the setting and context; we may become more descriptive to bring life to the story, but the basic story remains the same. In this way we are allowing God to speak through that story to others as they listen with their own hearts. They may receive a different message than we do – their message.

Even children can draw parallels with real life when hearing the **telling** of the Biblical story.

Two weeks after telling the parable of the treasure in the field in Christian Education class at our mission school, an eight year old came to me for clarification.

"Ms. Ruth, I want to talk to you about that man who bought that field in the Bible." I thought for a moment - then remembered the parable he was referring to. I encouraged him to tell me what was on his mind. "Well", he said, "he ripped that guy off!" I was puzzled and asked what he meant. "That guy knew there was a treasure in that field.....he should have been honest. He should have told the owner he had a treasure in his field. Instead, he just hurried up and bought it so he could get rich. He ripped him off!"

SESSION TWO: Telling

It dawned on me how that story connected with his life. He heard the stories about outsiders who years ago came to the mountains and bought up coal rights for pennies an acre. And, he had been told of the high value of that same coal today.

The **telling** of the Biblical story engaged his imagination and he connected it to his own life.

More good news! The most important step in becoming a good storyteller is to know the story so well it becomes a part of you. You may not have been aware, but during the first session of this journey as you read and re-read and pondered the story of Lydia you were doing just that!

There are no magic formulas, but there are some steps that can be helpful:

Ask God to guide you and to give you confidence.

1. Read, re-read! Ponder! Read aloud. Re-read aloud with expression. Pay attention to the characters in the story and what actions take place. Ask the who, what, when, where questions as you read.

2. Close your eyes and visualize the story in your mind.

3. Research words you don't know. Research the setting and context in which this story took place. (More good news – you've done that!)

4. Tell the story to yourself. Do this more than once.

5. Now, write out the story.

    ✝ Develop your introduction. You may want to include something about the context, the setting, the time the story took place.

    ✝ Develop the body of the story. Use descriptive words to paint a picture for the listener. Remember the who, what, when, where of the story and the order of events as you do this.

    ✝ Develop the ending. End the story as the Biblical story ends. Remember, we change words, not the story. Resist the temptation to add on a "and they lived happily ever after" (conclusion) type ending.

6. Critique what you have written. Make needed changes.

7. Now, tell the story aloud several times. Practice on another person.

8. Decide on what objects or methods you might employ.

9. Enjoy the telling!

SESSION TWO: Telling

When I first began telling the Biblical story, I worried about accuracy and about leaving something out of the story. It was helpful to me to use a chart to make an outline of the who, what, when and where questions.

TIME	PLACE	CHARACTERS	OBJECTS	ACTIONS

I also use 3x5 cards with a key phrase on each, stacked in the order the story is told to practice telling the story aloud.

You may find it helpful to use some object in **telling** the story, or you may want to use pictures or do a power-point presentation. You may want to tell the story through the voice of one of the characters. Use your imagination.

However, remember in telling, we do not change the story. You will be able to become more imaginative as you do **re-telling**.

RE-TELLING

In **re-telling**, the *storyteller* engages much more imagination. The story retains the basic concept, but is often cast in a different time and place, the characters may be fictitious or present-day, and often the story is embellished. As the story unfolds, the listener may say, "Ah ha!" That is like the Bible story about..."

For an example, the re-telling of the parable of the lost sheep might look like this:

Sunday afternoon. Must hurry up the road to pick up Mama Laura. We're due on Elk Creek by 2:00. She's ready. Has a bundle of kindling. The Bibles and other supplies are in my bag. We're off across the mountains doing our "Suitcase Sunday School".

Lots of houses – lots of children. Only a couple little churches. Preaching, but nothing for the children. Mama Laura says they need a Sunday School. So, we go. We use the old one-room school house. Rocks for steps and a pot bellied stove to keep warm.

The children don't mind. They've taught me a thing or two. How to kindle a fire, for one thing! And how to smack "warnuts" with rocks.

Eighteen miles – we're here! Watch for the children. How many will be on the road today?

SESSION TWO: Re-Telling

Smith's must have gone to their Granny's for the day.
The Phillips' have the flu.
There's Debbie running down the hillside! She sees us coming.
None of the Birchfield boys on the road.

What, only Debbie today? This is the third Sunday in a row. Only Debbie!

She never misses. She's eight. Lives with her MaMaw. MaMaw is old. Can't see; can't do much. Debbie takes home extra story papers to read to MaMaw.

Mama Laura! Mama Laura! I have a question. I have a question. Do you think God is trying to tell us some thing? Should we be spending our time somewhere else? It's a long way up here! Look! There's only Debbie!"

I see tears welling in her eyes. Hear the earnestness in her voice.

"Honey, as long as there is ONE child standing along this road – God WANTS us HERE! One child counts in the Kingdom!"

I'll not ask that question again.

Now, it's your turn. Remember the good news – you have already read and re-read and pondered the story in Session One. Secondly, the story has become part of you. You are ready to write out your own **telling and re-telling** of the story!

My Telling
Story of Lydia

_____

_____

_____

_____

_____

_____

_____

_____

_____

_____

_____

_____

_____

_____

_____

_____

_____

_____

_____

Lydia Ruth's Treasure Map

SESSION TWO: Telling

My Re-Telling
Story of Lydia

_____

_____

_____

_____

_____

_____

_____

_____

_____

_____

_____

_____

_____

_____

_____

_____

_____

SESSION TWO: Re-telling

_____

_____

_____

_____

_____

_____

_____

_____

_____

_____

_____

_____

_____

_____

_____

_____

_____

_____

_____

Group Time Session Two

In this second group time, focus on telling and re-telling your stories with one another, and on any discoveries you've made through the storytelling process.

When you gather:

Determine the total length of time the group will meet.

Look at the questions for discussion. You may want to add others.

Calculate the approximate time you will allow for telling and retelling, and also the time you will need for the questions, based on the total time you plan to meet.

Assign a time-keeper to keep the group on schedule.

Covenant with each other to be certain every participant has equal opportunity to share.

Agree to a signal to alert each other when someone becomes too lengthy and it is time for someone else to speak.

As you begin the sharing time:

Pray together, and ask the Holy Spirit to be among you.

Share your stories with one another.

After everyone has had the opportunity to share, consider the following questions together.

SESSION TWO: Group Time

Questions:

Did you receive any additional insights from the story when you heard it told by others?

_____

_____

_____

_____

_____

_____

_____

_____

_____

_____

_____

_____

_____

_____

_____

What have you discovered in the process of learning to tell and re-tell a Biblical story?

_____

_____

_____

_____

_____

_____

_____

What is the most difficult part of storytelling for you?

_____

_____

_____

_____

_____

_____

_____

_____

SESSION TWO: Group Time

Which is easier, telling, or re-telling? Why?

_____

_____

_____

_____

_____

_____

_____

How important do you feel it is that people learn to tell the Biblical story? Describe.

_____

_____

_____

_____

_____

_____

_____

The Treasure Map will challenge you to apply the treasures you find in the story of Lydia to your own life.

Session Three

You have pondered and researched the Biblical story of Lydia. You have learned to tell and re-tell the story. You have shared your journey with other travelers. You have heard about their journeys. And, all the while, you have been listening for God's message for you – seeking your own spiritual treasures from God within this story.

Looking back, remembering the journey, can help us connect the story from the Bible with our own life, and help us to respond to what God has revealed.

Review the first two sessions of this journey. Re-read your notes and comments.

What insights and treasures do they reveal? List them.

_____

_____

_____

_____

_____

_____

_____

_____

_____

_____

_____

_____

_____

_____

What personal message/treasure from God have you received?

_____

_____

_____

_____

_____

_____

_____

_____

_____

_____

_____

_____

_____

Is it what you expected? Elaborate.

_____

_____

_____

_____

_____

_____

_____

What might the discovery of your treasure(s) suggest
for your on-going journey of life?

_____

_____

_____

_____

_____

_____

_____

As you learned about Lydia, what qualities/characteristics did you see in her? List them.

_____

_____

_____

_____

_____

_____

Who in your life comes to mind as you look at this list? How was that characteristic demonstrated in their life?

_____

_____

_____

_____

_____

_____

_____

In what way has this influenced your life?

_____

_____

_____

_____

_____

_____

Which of Lydia's characteristics do you feel you have? Which would you LIKE to have?

_____

_____

_____

_____

_____

_____

_____

People come to a personal relationship with Jesus Christ in different ways. What do you think was the key to Lydia's conversion?

_____

_____

_____

_____

_____

_____

How does Lydia's experience compare with your own experience of Jesus Christ?

_____

_____

_____

_____

_____

_____

_____

Who have been the "Paul-persons" in your life who helped "open the Gospel" to you?

_____

_____

_____

_____

_____

_____

_____

_____

_____

_____

_____

_____

_____

In what way(s) did they do so?

_____

_____

_____

_____

_____

_____

_____

_____

_____

_____

_____

_____

_____

_____

_____

_____

_____

_____

_____

You have come to end of the beginning of the rest of your spiritual journey.

Did you make earthshaking discoveries? Lightening bolts fall from the sky? Did God speak through burning bushes all along your journey?

Probably not. In fact, you may feel a bit like Anthony.

Kindergartners were learning about Abraham's call from God to go to the Promised Land. After the storytelling the children were asked to draw a picture about the story.

Anita, with great animation, was trying to answer Anthony's question: "What does God look like anyway?

Christian Education class was Anthony's first exposure to Bible stories and God. Anita, however, regularly attended a small independent church and had many times heard the preached with passion.

With the great confidence of a 5 year old, she said, "Well, I don't know EXACTLY what God looks like, but I can tell you this, Anthony – the devil is on one shoulder God on the other, and they're fightin' over us."

Anthony stared at her for a while, then proceeded to circle around Anita, looking closely at her shoulders. He turned to me and said, "Ms. Ruth, I can't see either one of 'em, and I really want to see God to know what he looks like."

SESSION THREE

All I could say at the moment was, "Maybe you can't quite see God today, Anthony, but don't stop looking. One day you will see God clearly."

Anthony is a young adult by now. I'm not sure where he is, but I pray that in his life journey the search continued and he found God, right on his own shoulder!

So may it be for you!

NOTE: *Gather the supplies listed on pages 74-76 for the* ***Remember Lydia*** *project before meeting for Group Session III.*

Group Time Session Three

In this third group time, focus on sharing the treasures you have received from God during the study and how you will respond to God's message(s) for you.

When you gather:

Determine the total length of time the group will meet.

Assign a time-keeper to keep the group on schedule.

Covenant with each other to be sure every participant has equal opportunity to share.

Agree to a signal to alert each other when someone becomes too lengthy and it is time for someone else to speak.

SESSION THREE: Group Time

As you begin the sharing time:

     Pray together, and ask the Holy Spirit to be among you.

     Share with each other your message(s) from God and what affect that may have on your life.

     Share with each other about one person who helped open the Gospel to you.

We do not journey alone. God goes with us. God also works through other travelers we meet along the way. Pay attention to them, they may have treasures from God to share.

As a closing celebration, work together on the **Remember Lydia** project. Make one for yourself. Place it somewhere as a reminder of this journey.

Make another for one of the persons you named in this session who influenced your spiritual growth. Tell them about the journey you have been on, your discoveries, and acknowledge how they have touched your life. This can be done in person or through correspondence.

In closing, share with each other how you plan to incorporate your learnings – your message from God – into your life. Ask God, through the Holy Spirit, to guide each one's journey.

NOTE: When you have completed your journey, turn to the back page of the book to find a Secret Letter.

REMEMBER LYDIA

"Seller of Purple" Satin Pillow

Supplies:

1 package of purple satin blanket binding
purple fabric to make 2 squares, 13" each
poly soft loft batting for filling

How to:

Cut two 13" squares from fabric.
Cut blanket binding into twelve strips, 13" long each

Lay 6 of the strips vertically across one square.
Pin down all binding ends to fabric edge.
Weave the other 6 strips horizontally across.
Pin down all binding ends to fabric edge.

Position second square of fabric, right side down, over woven piece. Be sure edges are lined up with the 13" square under the woven section.
Pin down in several places to keep from shifting when you sew.

Draw a 12" square with pencil on the top fabric. (You will be leaving a 1" edge all the way around)

Sew three sides along the pencil line.
Sew the remaining side in only 2" from each end, (backstitch to hold firm).

Carefully turn the woven side out.
Stuff lightly with polyester batting.
Turn under seam allowance and sew the opening shut.

The pillow is elegant by itself, but you may add bows or other decorations.

"Seller of Purple" Sachet

(This is simply a smaller version of the pattern above.)

Supplies:

52" of 1" wide satin purple ribbon

    (or 26" purple and 26" lavender)

Purple fabric to make 2 squares, 6" each

Poly soft loft batting for filling

Dried lavender or your choice

How to:

Cut two 6" squares from fabric

Cut ribbon into 10 strips, 5" long each

Follow the directions for pillow, except draw a 5" square with pencil on top fabric, leaving 1" all around.

Sew in only 1" from edges on fourth side to enable stuffing.

Add small amount of dried lavender (or other scent) in with the cotton filling.

Sew the opening shut.

Pull heavy needle with heavy thread through center, draw up to form "pillow" effect.

Draw thread through several times, pulling snug.

Fasten thread.

Attach ribbon loop to one corner for hanging, if desired.

Lydia Ruth's Treasure Map

Finding Your Own Treasures in the Scriptures

Watch for the next five books by Ruth A. Wiertzema as she continues to lead Bible searchers on a journey through the lives of unique women found in the Scriptures.

About the Author

Ruth A. Wiertzema is a Diaconal Minister, Minnesota Conference, and a missionary of The United Methodist Church who has served the Red Bird Missionary Conference of Beverly, KY-the most comprehensive mission project of the UMC in the US-for 30 years. She is currently appointed as their Director of Connectional Ministries. Ruth was a former curriculum writer for the *One Room Sunday School* and also wrote the Christian Education section for Hinton Rural Life Center's *Models for Ministry*. UMW members will best recognize her as a mission interpreter, and churches will know her as editor of *The Cardinal*, a nationally distributed newsletter of the Red Bird Missionary Conference.

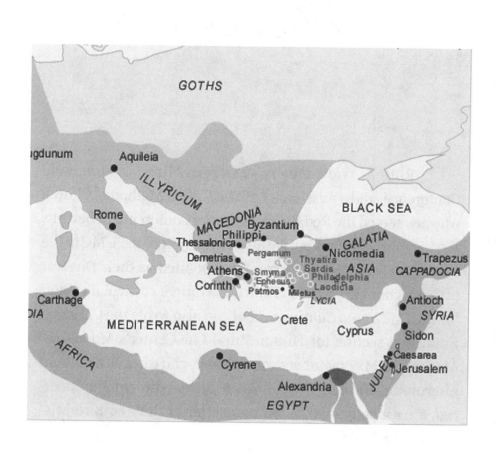

Turn the page to find
A Secret Letter
to travelers
on the journey

Dear Traveler,

Yes, I the author have been searching for treasures right along with you.

Two distinct messages came to me through the Biblical story of Lydia.

- God still speaks to open minds and an open hearts.
- From the time of the early Church, women have helped spread the Gospel.

Both of these messages are embodied in one of the most treasured experiences of my life.

I spoke on behalf of God's mission to a women's circle in Oklahoma. Most of the women were in the 30-40 year range, busy with families and jobs, and yet seeking spiritual enrichment.

These women became filled with passion and enthusiasm for mission. They began years of annual trips to Kentucky to help renovate a former Girl Scout camp given to Red Bird Mission.

Their enthusiasm spread. They even got their husbands involved. The women and men worked hard, laughed a lot, prayed a lot, and developed life-long spiritual bonds.

Lee was one of the husbands. While he had faith in God, regular involvement in the church had not been his pattern. In the beginning, he did not quite understand what this "mission" stuff was all about and why Donna was using her vacation time working in mission. But, he knew if he wanted to spend time with his wife, he best go along.

Lee is a contemplative, quiet, gentle man. His skills are many, and he engaged himself fully into the efforts. And he listened and observed. And he opened his heart.

Prior to the group's third annual trip, I received a phone call from Lee. I shall never forget it.

"Ruth, I know you're some kind of minister in the church. I'd like to ask you something. Can you baptize me?" I was totally taken off guard, and asked him to tell me more.

"Camp O'Cumberlands is holy ground for me. God and I have worked out some things there. I want to be baptized in the creek."

The water in Pearl Branch is anything but warm in April, but when Lee, two pastors and I got in, we felt seemed "strangely warmed". As he had requested, Lee was baptized in the creek running through his "holy ground." After that trip, Lee became an active member of their church in Illinois.

Though the genders of the people in the stories are reversed, I see parallels in Lydia's story and Lee's story.

In the Lydia story, the witness of Paul the missionary led to Lydia's conversion. It was the witness of women in mission that lead to Lee's commitment.

Lydia opened her door to start a church.   Mission service was the door that opened the church to Lee.

Both Lydia and Lee had open minds and open hearts to receive God's message.

This parallel confirmed two things for me: that the God of the Bible is the God of today; and just as in the early Church, women still play an important role in spreading the Gospel.

God's message to me is to keep my mind and heart so that I might recognize and respond to the opportunities given to me!

To God be the Glory!

with A. Wicaksono